Every Christmas, good boys and girls get presents from Santa Claus.

Naughty boys and girls find lumps of coal in their stockings . . .

For Logan

Carolrhoda Books
A division of Lerner Publishing Group, Inc.
241 First Avenue North
Minneapolis, MN 55401 USA

For reading levels and more information, look up this title at
www.lernerbooks.com.

Main body text set in ChurchwardSamoa 18/24.
Typeface provided by Chank.

Library of Congress Cataloging-in-Publication Data

Kulka, Joe, author, illustrator.
    The Christmas Coal Man / by Joe Kulka ; illustrated by Joe Kulka.
      pages cm
    Summary: Every year the Coal Man works hard to mine enough coal
for Santa's naughty list, but this year Santa tells him that he has decided
that he no longer needs coal.
    ISBN 978-1-4677-1607-9 (lib. bdg. : alk. paper)
    ISBN 978-1-4677-8808-3 (EB pdf)
    1. Christmas stories. 2. Coal miners—Juvenile fiction. 3. Coal—
Juvenile fiction. 4. Santa Claus—Juvenile fiction. [1. Christmas—Fiction.
2. Coal—Fiction. 3. Santa Claus—Fiction.] I. Title.
PZ7.K9490153Ch 2014
[E]—dc23   2013035167

Manufactured in the United States of America
1 - VI - 7/15/15

The Christmas Coal Man

Joe Kulka

 CAROLRHODA BOOKS MINNEAPOLIS

Deep inside a coal mine, a little man swung his pickaxe against a damp wall.

He chipped away at black rock, carefully placing the shiniest pieces of coal into a bag marked

Xmas Coal.

Soon he would deliver the coal to the North Pole, as he did every year.

"We did good today, Jenny," the Coal Man said, gently scratching his mule's ears. "There's some real choice pieces of coal in that bag." He wiped his brow and handed the mule a carrot.

The Coal Man's canary let out a tired peep. The Coal Man stretched his aching back as he loaded the coal behind Jenny. Together, they headed to his cabin for the night.

The Coal Man tapped the picture of the tropical island on his calendar and smiled. "Someday, Jenny, you'll do no more heavy lifting. We'll just stroll down the beach all day long." Jenny snorted softly.

The Coal Man sprinkled a handful of sunflower seeds into the canary's cage. "Someday, Pete, you'll fly above the palm trees."

"Someday . . . but not yet." The Coal Man peered into the coffee can where he kept his earnings. Still not enough to move to a tropical island. Troubles kept dipping into their savings—veterinarian bills for Pete, broken pickaxes, new shoes for Jenny.

"We still have a lot of work to do," the Coal Man said. "Christmas is coming fast, and we have more coal to dig."

After a few more weeks of hard work, the Coal Man had stacked burlap sacks to the mine's upper timbers. He tallied up the black lumps. "Yep. We got enough for this year." His face lit up. "Tomorrow, we are heading to the North Pole!"

Snow fell gently as Jenny struggled up a steep hill. "We're getting closer to Santa's workshop. The snow is probably going to get heavier," the Coal Man said. He put a thick quilt around Pete's cage. "Someday we won't need this, Pete. You'll be flying around in tropical breezes."

The northern lights danced in the sky as the Coal Man placed his bags onto the loading dock at Santa's workshop.

"Santa wants to talk with you," said the elf that signed for the delivery. "Go ahead inside. I'll put Jenny in the stables with the reindeer, and we have some sunflower seeds for Pete."

The Coal Man fiddled with the lamp on his hat and stared at his boots. "Santa wants to talk to me?" he asked.

"He's right inside," the elf said. "Go on in."

"Coal Man!" Santa boomed. "Great to see you. Have a seat!" Santa patted the Coal Man on his knee. "I'm afraid I have bad news. Starting this Christmas, I'm not giving out coal anymore. My naughty list stays about the same length every year. The whole coal-in-the-stocking thing just isn't working."

The Coal Man was speechless.

NAUGHTY

Michael

James

Kaitlyn

Logan

Stevie

Tommy

Anna

Frances

"I need a new approach. Instead of something bad for naughty boys and girls, something extra special for REALLY good boys and girls. Now maybe the naughty children will try harder to be good. I'm not sure exactly what I'll give yet, but it certainly won't be coal. I'm sorry."

"But . . . what am I supposed to do?" stammered the Coal Man.

"I've heard you say that you'd like to go somewhere warm. Why don't you do that?" Santa's eyes twinkled as he handed Coal Man back one of his coal bags. "You'll want to keep this as a reminder of all the years we worked together. Take care."

"I don't think we will be retiring anytime soon, Jenny," the Coal Man said. "At least we can use this coal for a nice campfire."

He reached into the bag for a few lumps but slipped on a patch of ice. The bag of rocks spilled everywhere.

The Coal Man inspected the clumps in the snow. They sparkled back at him.

"This isn't coal! These are diamonds!" The Coal Man danced for joy. "Hey, Jenny! Pete! Do you know what today is? It's SOMEDAY!"

The Coal Man still works for Santa, but his job is much easier. Now he combs the beach, finding unusual seashells for Santa.

Seashells that only the best good boys and girls get in their stockings.